Perilous Play, and, Lost in a Pyramid or the Mummy's Curse

Louisa May Alcott

DODO PRESS

Perilous Play

"If someone does not propose a new and interesting amusement, I shall die of ennui! " said pretty Belle Daventry, in a tone of despair. "I have read all my books, used up all my Berlin wools, and it's too warm to go to town for more. No one can go sailing yet, as the tide is out; we are all nearly tired to death of cards, croquet, and gossip, so what shall we do to while away this endless afternoon? Dr. Meredith, I command you to invent and propose a new game in five minutes. "

"To hear is to obey, " replied the young man, who lay in the grass at her feet, as he submissively slapped his forehead, and fell a-thinking with all his might.

Holding up her finger to preserve silence, Belle pulled out her watch and waited with an expectant smile. The rest of the young party, who were indolently scattered about under the elms, drew nearer, and brightened visibly, for Dr. Meredith's inventive powers were well-known, and something refreshingly novel might be expected from him. One gentleman did not stir, but then he lay within earshot, and merely turned his fine eyes from the sea to the group before him. His glance rested a moment on Belle's piquant figure, for she looked very pretty with her bright hair blowing in the wind, one plump white arm extended to keep order, and one little foot, in a distracting slipper, just visible below the voluminous folds of her dress. Then the glance passed to another figure, sitting somewhat apart in a cloud of white muslin, for an airy burnoose floated from head and shoulders, showing only a singularly charming face. Pale and yet brilliant, for the Southern eyes were magnificent, the clear olive cheeks contrasted well with darkest hair; lips like a pomegranate flower, and delicate, straight brows, as mobile as the lips. A cluster of crimson flowers, half falling from the loose black braids, and a golden bracelet of Arabian coins on the slender wrist were the only ornaments she wore, and became her better than the fashionable frippery of her companions. A book lay on her lap, but her eyes, full of a passionate melancholy, were fixed on the sea, which glittered around an island green and flowery as a summer paradise. Rose St. Just was as beautiful as her Spanish mother, but had inherited the pride and reserve of her English father; and this pride was the thorn which repelled lovers from the human flower. Mark Done sighed as he looked, and as if the sigh, low as it was, roused her from her reverie, Rose flashed a quick glance at him, took up her book, and went on reading the legend of "The Lotus Eaters. "

"Time is up now, Doctor, " cried Belle, pocketing her watch with a flourish.

"Ready to report, " answered Meredith, sitting up and producing a little box of tortoiseshell and gold.

"How mysterious! What is it? Let me see, first! " And Belle removed the cover, looking like an inquisitive child.

"Only bonbons; how stupid! That won't do, sir. We don't want to be fed with sugar-plums. We demand to be amused."

"Eat six of these despised bonbons, and you will be amused in a new, delicious, and wonderful manner," said the young doctor, laying half a dozen on a green leaf and offering them to her.

"Why, what are they?" she asked, looking at him askance.

"Hashish; did you never hear of it?"

"Oh, yes; it's that Indian stuff which brings one fantastic visions, isn't it? I've always wanted to see and taste it, and now I will," cried Belle, nibbling at one of the bean-shaped comfits with its green heart.

"I advise you not to try it. People do all sorts of queer things when they take it. I wouldn't for the world," said a prudent young lady warningly, as all examined the box and its contents.

"Six can do no harm, I give you my word. I take twenty before I can enjoy myself, and some people even more. I've tried many experiments, both on the sick and the well, and nothing ever happened amiss, though the demonstrations were immensely interesting," said Meredith, eating his sugar-plums with a tranquil air, which was very convincing to others.

"How shall I feel? " asked Belle, beginning on her second comfit.

"A heavenly dreaminess comes over one, in which they move as if on air. Everything is calm and lovely to them: no pain, no care, no fear of anything, and while it lasts one feels like an angel half asleep. "

"But if one takes too much, how then? " said a deep voice behind the doctor.

"Hum! Well, that's not so pleasant, unless one likes phantoms, frenzies, and a touch of nightmare, which seems to last a thousand years. Ever try it, Done? " replied Meredith, turning toward the speaker, who was now leaning on his arm and looking interested.

"Never. I'm not a good subject for experiments. Too nervous a temperament to play pranks with. "

"I should say ten would be about your number. Less than that seldom affects men. Ladies go off sooner, and don't need so many. Miss St. Just, may I offer you a taste of Elysium? I owe my success to you, " said the doctor, approaching her deferentially.

"To me! And how? " she asked, lifting her large eyes with a slight smile.

"I was in the depths of despair when my eye caught the title of your book, and I was saved. For I remembered that I had hashish in my pocket. "

"Are you a lotus-eater? " she said, permitting him to lay the six charmed bonbons on the page.

"My faith, no! I use it for my patients. It is very efficacious in nervous disorders, and is getting to be quite a pet remedy with us. "

"I do not want to forget the past, but to read the future. Will hashish help me to do that? " asked Rose with an eager look, which made the young man flush, wondering if he bore any part in her hopes of that veiled future.

"Alas, no. I wish it could, for I, too, long to know my fate, " he answered, very low, as he looked into the lovely face before him.

The soft glance changed to one of cool indifference and Rose gently brushed the hashish off her book, saying, with a little gesture of dismissal, "Then I have no desire to taste Elysium. "

The white morsels dropped into the grass at her feet; but Dr. Meredith let them lie, and turning sharply, went back to sun himself in Belle's smiles.

"I've eaten all mine, and so has Evelyn. Mr. Norton will see goblins, I know, for he has taken quantities. I'm glad of it, for he does not believe in it, and I want to have him convinced by making a spectacle of himself for our amusement, " said Belle, in great spirits at the new plan.

"When does the trance come on? " asked Evelyn, a shy girl, already rather alarmed at what she had done.

"About three hours after you take your dose, though the time varies with different people. Your pulse will rise, heart beat quickly, eyes darken and dilate, and an uplifted sensation will pervade you generally. Then these symptoms change, and the bliss begins. I've seen people sit or lie in one position for hours, rapt in a delicious dream, and wake from it as tranquil as if they had not a nerve in their bodies. "

"How charming! I'll take some every time I'm worried. Let me see. It's now four, so our trances will come about seven, and we will devote the evening to manifestations, " said Belle.

"Come, Done, try it. We are all going in for the fun. Here's your dose, " and Meredith tossed him a dozen bonbons, twisted up in a bit of paper.

"No, thank you; I know myself too well to risk it. If you are all going to turn hashish-eaters, you'll need someone to take care of you, so I'll keep sober, " tossing the little parcel back.

It fell short, and the doctor, too lazy to pick it up, let it lie, merely saying, with a laugh, "Well, I advise any bashful man to take hashish when he wants to offer his heart to any fair lady, for it will give him the courage of a hero, the eloquence of a poet, and the ardor of an Italian.

Remember that, gentlemen, and come to me when the crisis approaches. "

"Does it conquer the pride, rouse the pity, and soften the hard hearts of the fair sex? " asked Done.

"I dare say now is your time to settle the fact, for here are two ladies who have imbibed, and in three hours will be in such a seraphic state of mind that 'No' will be an impossibility to them. "

"Oh, mercy on us; what have we done? If that's the case, I shall shut myself up till my foolish fit is over. Rose, you haven't taken any; I beg you to mount guard over me, and see that I don't disgrace myself by any nonsense. Promise me you will, " cried Belle, in half-real, half-feigned alarm at the consequences of her prank.

"I promise, " said Rose, and floated down the green path as noiselessly as a white cloud, with a curious smile on her lips.

"Don't tell any of the rest what we have done, but after tea let us go into the grove and compare notes, " said Norton, as Done strolled away to the beach, and the voices of approaching friends broke the summer quiet.

At tea, the initiated glanced covertly at one another, and saw, or fancied they saw, the effects of the hashish, in a certain suppressed excitement of manner, and unusually brilliant eyes. Belle laughed often, a silvery ringing laugh, pleasant to hear; but when complimented on her good spirits, she looked distressed and said she could not help her merriment; Meredith was quite calm, but rather dreamy; Evelyn was pale, and her next neighbor heard her heart beat; Norton talked incessantly, but as he talked uncommonly well, no one suspected anything. Done and Miss St. Just watched the others with interest, and were very quiet, especially Rose, who scarcely spoke, but smiled her sweetest, and looked very lovely.

The moon rose early, and the experimenters slipped away to the grove, leaving the outsiders on the lawn as usual. Some bold spirit asked Rose to sing, and she at once complied, pouring out Spanish airs in a voice that melted the hearts of her audience, so full of fiery sweetness or tragic pathos was it. Done seemed quite carried away, and lay with his face in the grass, to hide the tears that would come; till, afraid of openly disgracing himself, he started up and hurried down to the little wharf, where he sat alone, listening to the music with a countenance which plainly revealed to the stars the passion which possessed him. The sound of loud laughter from the grove, followed by entire silence, caused him to wonder what demonstrations were taking place, and half resolve to go and see. But that enchanting voice held him captive, even when a boat put off mysteriously from a point nearby, and sailed away like a phantom through the twilight.

Half an hour afterward, a white figure came down the path, and Rose's voice broke in on his midsummer night's dream. The moon shone clearly now, and showed him the anxiety in her face as she said hurriedly, "Where is Belle? "

"Gone sailing, I believe. "

"How could you let her go? She was not fit to take care of herself! "

"I forgot that. "

"So did I, but I promised to watch over her, and I must. Which way did they go? " demanded Rose, wrapping the white mantle about her, and running her eye over the little boats moored below.

"You will follow her? "

"Yes. "

"I'll be your guide then. They went toward the lighthouse; it is too far to row; I am at your service. Oh, say yes, " cried Done, leaping into his own skiff and offering his hand persuasively.

She hesitated an instant and looked at him. He was always pale, and the moonlight seemed to increase this pallor, but his hat brim hid his eyes, and his voice was very quiet. A loud peal of laughter floated over the water, and as if the sound decided her, she gave him her hand and entered the boat. Done smiled triumphantly as he shook out the sail, which caught the freshening wind, and sent the boat dancing along a path of light.

How lovely it was! All the indescribable allurements of a perfect summer night surrounded them: balmy airs, enchanting moonlight, distant music, and, close at hand, the delicious atmosphere of love, which made itself felt in the eloquent silences that fell between them. Rose seemed to yield to the subtle charm, and leaned back on the cushioned seat with her beautiful head uncovered, her face full of dreamy softness, and her hands lying loosely clasped before her. She seldom spoke, showed no further anxiety for Belle, and soon seemed to forget the object of her search, so absorbed was she in some delicious thought which wrapped her in its peace.

Done sat opposite, flushed now, restless, and excited, for his eyes glittered; the hand on the rudder shook, and his voice sounded intense and passionate, even in the utterance of the simplest words. He talked continually and with unusual brilliancy, for, though a man of many accomplishments, he was too indolent or too fastidious to exert himself, except among his peers. Rose seemed to look without seeing, to listen without hearing, and though she smiled blissfully, the smiles were evidently not for him.

On they sailed, scarcely heeding the bank of black cloud piled up in the horizon, the rising wind, or the silence which proved their solitude. Rose moved once or twice, and lifted her hand as if to speak, but sank back mutely, and the hand fell again as if it had not energy enough to enforce her wish. A cloud sweeping over the moon, a distant growl of thunder, and the slight gust that struck the sail seemed to rouse her. Done was singing now like one inspired, his hat at his feet, hair in disorder, and a strangely rapturous expression in his eyes, which were fixed on her. She started, shivered, and seemed to recover herself with an effort.

"Where are they? " she asked, looking vainly for the island heights and the other boat.

"They have gone to the beach, I fancy, but we will follow. " As Done leaned forward to speak, she saw his face and shrank back with a sudden flush, for in it she read clearly what she had felt, yet doubted until now. He saw the telltale blush and gesture, and said impetuously, "You know it now; you cannot deceive me longer, or daunt me with your pride! Rose, I love you, and dare tell you so tonight! "

"Not now—not here—I will not listen. Turn back, and be silent, I entreat you, Mr. Done, " she said hurriedly.

He laughed a defiant laugh and took her hand in his, which was burning and throbbing with the rapid heat of his pulse.

"No, I will have my answer here, and now, and never turn back till you give it; you have been a thorny Rose, and given me many wounds. I'll be paid for my heartache with sweet words, tender looks, and frank confessions of love, for proud as you are, you do love me, and dare not deny it. "

Something in his tone terrified her; she snatched her hand away and drew beyond his reach, trying to speak calmly, and to meet coldly the ardent glances of the eyes which were strangely darkened and dilated with uncontrollable emotion.

"You forget yourself. I shall give no answer to an avowal made in such terms. Take me home instantly, " she said in a tone of command.

"Confess you love me, Rose. "

"Never! "

"Ah! I'll have a kinder answer, or—" Done half rose and put out his hand to grasp and draw her to him, but the cry she uttered seemed to arrest him with a sort of shock. He dropped into his seat, passed his hand over his eyes, and shivered nervously as he muttered in an altered tone, "I meant nothing; it's the moonlight; sit down, I'll control myself—upon my soul I will! "

"If you do not, I shall go overboard. Are you mad, sir? " cried Rose, trembling with indignation.

"Then I shall follow you, for I am mad, Rose, with love—hashish! "

His voice sank to a whisper, but the last word thrilled along her nerves, as no sound of fear had ever done before. An instant she regarded him with a look which took in every sign of unnatural excitement, then she clasped her hands with an imploring gesture, saying, in a tone of despair, "Why did I come? How will it end? Oh, Mark, take me home before it is too late! "

"Hush! Be calm; don't thwart me, or I may get wild again. My thoughts are not clear, but I understand you. There, take my knife, and if I forget myself, kill me. Don't go overboard; you are too beautiful to die, my Rose! "

He threw her the slender hunting-knife he wore, looked at her a moment with a far-off look, and trimmed the sail like one moving in a dream. Rose took the weapon, wrapped her cloak closely about her, and crouching as far away as possible, kept her eye on him, with a face in which watchful terror contended with some secret trouble and bewilderment more powerful than her fear.

The boat moved round and begin to beat up against wind and tide; spray flew from her bow; the sail bent and strained in the gusts that struck it with perilous fitfulness. The moon was nearly hidden by scudding clouds, and one half the sky was black with the gathering storm. Rose looked from threatening heavens to treacherous sea, and tried to be ready for any danger, but her calm had been sadly broken, and she could not recover it. Done sat motionless, uttering no word of encouragement, though the frequent flaws almost tore the rope from his hand, and the water often dashed over him.

"Are we in any danger? " asked Rose at last, unable to bear the silence, for he looked like a ghostly helmsman seen by the fitful light, pale now, wild-eyed, and speechless.

"Yes, great danger. "

"I thought you were a skillful boatman. "

"I am when I am myself; now I am rapidly losing the control of my will, and the strange quiet is coming over me. If I had been alone I should have given up sooner, but for your sake I've kept on. "

"Can't you work the boat? " asked Rose, terror-struck by the changed tone of his voice, the slow, uncertain movements of his hands.

"No. I see everything through a thick cloud; your voice sounds far away, and my one desire is to lay my head down and sleep. "

"Let me steer—I can, I must! " she cried, springing toward him and laying her hand on the rudder.

He smiled and kissed the little hand, saying dreamily, "You could not hold it a minute; sit by me, love; let us turn the boat again, and drift away together—anywhere, anywhere out of the world. "

"Oh, heaven, what will become of us! " and Rose wrung her hands in real despair. "Mr. Done—Mark—dear Mark, rouse yourself and listen to me. Turn, as you say, for it is certain death to go on. Turn, and let us drift down to the lighthouse; they will hear and help us. Quick, take down the sail, get out the oars, and let us try to reach there before the storm breaks. "

As Rose spoke, he obeyed her like a dumb animal; love for her was stronger even than the instinct of self-preservation, and for her sake he fought against the treacherous lethargy which was swiftly overpowering him. The sail was lowered, the boat brought round, and with little help from the ill-pulled oars it drifted rapidly out to sea with the ebbing tide.

As she caught her breath after this dangerous maneuver was accomplished, Rose asked, in a quiet tone she vainly tried to render natural, "How much hashish did you take? "

"All that Meredith threw me. Too much; but I was possessed to do it, so I hid the roll and tried it, " he answered, peering at her with a weird laugh.

"Let us talk; our safety lies in keeping awake, and I dare not let you sleep, " continued Rose, dashing water on her own hot forehead with a sort of desperation.

"Say you love me; that would wake me from my lost sleep, I think. I have hoped and feared, waited and suffered so long. Be pitiful, and answer, Rose. "

"I do; but I should not own it now. "

So low was the soft reply he scarcely heard it, but he felt it and made a strong effort to break from the hateful spell that bound him. Leaning forward, he tried to read her face in a ray of moonlight breaking through the clouds; he saw a new and tender warmth in it, for all the pride was gone, and no fear marred the eloquence of those soft, Southern eyes.

"Kiss me, Rose, then I shall believe it. I feel lost in a dream, and you, so changed, so kind, may be only a fair phantom. Kiss me, love, and make it real. "

As if swayed by a power more potent than her will, Rose bent to meet his lips. But the ardent pressure seemed to startle her from a momentary oblivion of everything but love. She covered up her face and sank down, as if overwhelmed with shame, sobbing through passionate tears, "Oh, what am I doing? I am mad, for I, too, have taken hashish! "

What he answered she never heard, for a rattling peal of thunder drowned his voice, and then the storm broke loose. Rain fell in torrents, the wind blew fiercely, sky and sea were black as ink, and the boat tossed from wave to wave almost at their mercy. Giving herself up for lost, Rose crept to her lover's side and clung there, conscious only that they would bide together through the perils their own folly brought them. Done's excitement was quite gone now; he sat like a statue, shielding the frail creature whom he loved with a smile on his face, which looked awfully emotionless when the lightning gave her glimpses of its white immobility. Drenched, exhausted, and half senseless with danger, fear, and exposure, Rose saw at last a welcome glimmer through the gloom, and roused herself to cry for help.

"Mark, wake and help me! Shout, for God's sake—shout and call them, for we are lost if we drift by! " she cried, lifting his head from his breast, and forcing him to see the brilliant beacons streaming far across the troubled water.

He understood her, and springing up, uttered shout after shout like one demented. Fortunately, the storm had lulled a little; the lighthouse keeper heard and answered. Rose seized the helm, Done the oars, and with one frantic effort guided the boat into quieter waters, where it was met by the keeper, who towed it to the rocky nook which served as harbor.

The moment a strong, steady face met her eyes, and a gruff, cheery voice hailed her, Rose gave way, and was carried up to the house, looking more like a beautiful drowned Ophelia than a living woman.

"Here, Sally, see to the poor thing; she's had a rough time on't. I'll take care of her sweetheart—and a nice job I'll have, I reckon, for if he ain't mad or drunk, he's had a stroke of lightnin', and looks as if he wouldn't get his hearin' in a hurry, " said the old man as he housed his unexpected guests and stood staring at Done, who looked about him like one dazed. "You jest turn in younder and sleep it off, mate. We'll see to the lady, and right up your boat in the morning, " the old man added.

"Be kind to Rose. I frightened her. I'll not forget you. Yes, let me sleep and get over this cursed folly as soon as possible, " muttered this strange visitor.

Done threw himself down on the rough couch and tried to sleep, but every nerve was overstrained, every pulse beating like a trip-hammer, and everything about him was intensified and exaggerated with awful power. The thundershower seemed a wild hurricane, the quaint room a wilderness peopled with tormenting phantoms, and all the events of his life passed before him in an endless procession, which nearly maddened him. The old man looked weird and gigantic, his own voice sounded shrill and discordant, and the ceaseless murmur of Rose's incoherent wanderings haunted him like parts of a grotesque but dreadful dream.

All night he lay motionless, with staring eyes, feverish lips, and a mind on the rack, for the delicate machinery which had been tampered with revenged the wrong by torturing the foolish experimenter. All night Rose wept and sang, talked and cried for help in a piteous state of nervous excitement, for with her the trance came first, and the after-agitation was increased by the events of the evening. She slept at last, lulled by the old woman's motherly care, and Done was spared one tormenting fear, for he dreaded the consequences of this folly on her, more than upon himself.

As day dawned he rose, haggard and faint, and staggered out. At the door he met the keeper, who stopped him to report that the boat was in order, and a fair day coming. Seeing doubt and perplexity in the old man's eye, Done told him the truth, and added that he was going to the beach for a plunge, hoping by that simple tonic to restore his unstrung nerves.

He came back feeling like himself again, except for a dull headache, and a heavy sense of remorse weighing on his spirits, for he distinctly recollected all the events of the night. The old woman made him eat and drink, and in an hour he felt ready for the homeward trip.

Rose slept late, and when she woke soon recovered herself, for her dose had been a small one. When she had breakfasted and made a hasty toilet, she professed herself anxious to return at once. She dreaded yet longed to see Done, and when the time came armed herself with pride, feeling all a woman's shame at what had passed, and resolving to feign forgetfulness of the incidents of the previous night. Pale and cold as a statue she met him, but the moment he began to say humbly, "Forgive me, Rose," she silenced him with an imperious gesture and the command, "Don't speak of it; I only remember that it was very horrible, and wish to forget it all as soon as possible."

"All, Rose? " he added, significantly.

"Yes, all. No one would care to recall the follies of a hashish dream, " she answered, turning hastily to hide the scarlet flush that would rise, and the eyes that would fall before his own.

"I never can forget, but I will be silent if you bid me. "

"I do. Let us go. What will they think at the island? Mr. Done, give me your promise to tell no one, now or ever, that I tried that dangerous experiment. I will guard your secret also. " She spoke eagerly and looked up imploringly.

"I promise, " and he gave her his hand, holding her own with a wistful glance, till she drew it away and begged him to take her home.

Leaving hearty thanks and a generous token of their gratitude, they sailed away with a fair wind, finding in the freshness of the morning a speedy cure for tired bodies and excited minds. They said little, but it was impossible for Rose to preserve her coldness. The memory of the past night broke down her pride, and Done's tender glances touched her heart. She half hid her face behind her hand, and tried to compose herself for the scene to come, for as she approached the island, she saw Belle and her party waiting for them on the shore.

"Oh, Mr. Done, screen me from their eyes and questions as much as you can! I'm so worn out and nervous, I shall betray myself. You will help me? " And she turned to him with a confiding look, strangely at variance with her usual calm self-possession.

"I'll shield you with my life, if you will tell me why you took the hashish, " he said, bent on knowing his fate.

"I hoped it would make me soft and lovable, like other women. I'm tired of being a lonely statue, " she faltered, as if the truth was wrung from her by a power stronger than her will.

"And I took it to gain courage to tell my love. Rose, we have been near death together; let us share life together, and neither of us be any more lonely or afraid? "

He stretched his hand to her with his heart in his face, and she gave him hers with a look of tender submission, as he said ardently, "Heaven bless hashish, if its dreams end like this! "

THE END

Lost in a Pyramid or the Mummy's Curse

I

"And what are these, Paul? " asked Evelyn, opening a tarnished gold box and examining its contents curiously.

"Seeds of some unknown Egyptian plant, " replied Forsyth, with a sudden shadow on his dark face, as he looked down at the three scarlet grains lying in the white hand lifted to him.

"Where did you get them? " asked the girl.

"That is a weird story, which will only haunt you if I tell it, " said Forsyth, with an absent expression that strongly excited the girl's curiosity.

"Please tell it, I like weird tales, and they never trouble me. Ah, do tell it; your stories are always so interesting, " she cried, looking up with such a pretty blending of entreaty and command in her charming face, that refusal was impossible.

"You'll be sorry for it, and so shall I, perhaps; I warn you beforehand, that harm is foretold to the possessor of those mysterious seeds, " said Forsyth, smiling, even while he knit his black brows, and regarded the blooming creature before him with a fond yet foreboding glance.

"Tell on, I'm not afraid of these pretty atoms, " she answered, with an imperious nod.

"To hear is to obey. Let me read the facts, and then I will begin, " returned Forsyth, pacing to and fro with the far-off look of one who turns the pages of the past.

Evelyn watched him a moment, and then returned to her work, or play, rather, for the task seemed well suited to the vivacious little creature, half-child, half-woman.

"While in Egypt, " commenced Forsyth, slowly, "I went one day with my guide and Professor Niles, to explore the Cheops. Niles had a mania for antiquities of all sorts, and forgot time, danger and fatigue in the ardor of his pursuit. We rummaged up and down the narrow passages, half choked with dust and close air; reading inscriptions on the walls, stumbling over shattered mummy-cases, or coming face to face with some shriveled specimen perched like a hobgoblin on the little shelves where the dead used to be stowed away for ages. I was desperately tired after a few hours of it, and begged the professor to return. But he was bent on exploring certain places, and would not desist. We had but one guide, so I was forced to stay; but Jumal, my man, seeing how weary I was, proposed to us to rest in one of the larger passages, while he went to procure another guide for Niles. We consented, and assuring us that we were perfectly safe, if we did not quit the spot, Jumal left us, promising to return speedily. The professor sat down to take notes of his researches, and stretching my self on the soft sand, I fell asleep.

"I was roused by that indescribable thrill which instinctively warns us of danger, and springing up, I found myself alone. One torch burned faintly where Jumal had struck it, but Niles and the other light were gone. A dreadful sense of loneliness oppressed me for a moment; then I collected myself and looked well about me. A bit of paper was pinned to my hat, which lay near me, and on it, in the professor's writing were these words:

"'I've gone back a little to refresh my memory on certain points. Don't follow me till Jumal comes. I can find my way back to you, for I have a clue. Sleep well, and dream gloriously of the Pharaohs. N N. '

"I laughed at first over the old enthusiast, then felt anxious then restless, and finally resolved to follow him, for I discovered a strong cord fastened to a fallen stone, and knew that this was the clue he spoke of. Leaving a line for Jumal, I took my torch and retraced my steps, following the cord along the winding ways. I often shouted, but received no reply, and pressed on, hoping at each turn to see the old man poring over some musty relic of antiquity. Suddenly the cord ended, and lowering my torch, I saw that the footsteps had gone on.

"'Rash fellow, he'll lose himself, to a certainty, ' I thought, really alarmed now.

"As I paused, a faint call reached me, and I answered it, waited, shouted again, and a still fainter echo replied.

"Niles was evidently going on, misled by the reverberations of the low passages. No time was to be lost, and, forgetting myself, I stuck my torch in the deep sand to guide me back to the clue, and ran down the straight path before me, whooping like a madman as I went. I did not mean to lose sight of the light, but in my eagerness to find Niles I turned from the main passage, and, guided by his voice, hastened on. His torch soon gladdened my eyes, and the clutch of his trembling hands told me what agony he had suffered.

"'Let us get out of this horrible place at once, ' he said, wiping the great drops off his forehead.

"'Come, we're not far from the clue. I can soon reach it, and then we are safe'; but as I spoke, a chill passed over me, for a perfect labyrinth of narrow paths lay before us.

"Trying to guide myself by such land-marks as I had observed in my hasty passage, I followed the tracks in the sand till I fancied we must be near my light. No glimmer appeared, however, and kneeling down to examine the footprints nearer, I discovered, to my dismay, that I had been following the wrong ones, for among those marked by a deep boot-heel, were prints of bare feet; we had had no guide there, and Jumal wore sandals.

"Rising, I confronted Niles, with the one despairing word, 'Lost! ' as I pointed from the treacherous sand to the fast-waning light.

"I thought the old man would be overwhelmed but, to my surprise, he grew quite calm and steady, thought a moment, and then went on, saying, quietly:

"'Other men have passed here before us; let us follow their steps, for, if I do not greatly err, they lead toward great passages, where one's way is easily found. '

"On we went, bravely, till a misstep threw the professor violently to the ground with a broken leg, and nearly extinguished the torch. It was a horrible predicament, and I gave up all hope as I sat beside the poor fellow, who lay exhausted with fatigue, remorse and pain, for I would not leave him.

"'Paul, ' he said suddenly, 'if you will not go on, there is one more effort we can make. I remember hearing that a party lost as we are, saved themselves by building a fire. The smoke penetrated further than sound or light, and the guide's quick wit understood the unusual mist; he followed it, and rescued the party. Make a fire and trust to Jumal. '

"'A fire without wood? ' I began; but he pointed to a shelf behind me, which had escaped me in the gloom; and on it I saw a slender mummy- case. I understood him, for these dry cases, which lie about in hundreds, are freely used as firewood. Reaching up, I pulled it down, believing it to be empty, but as it fell, it burst open, and out rolled a mummy. Accustomed as I was to such sights, it startled me a little, for danger had unstrung my nerves. Laying the little brown chrysalis aside, I smashed the case, lit the pile with my torch, and soon a light cloud of smoke drifted down the three passages which diverged from the cell-like place where we had paused.

"While busied with the fire, Niles, forgetful of pain and peril, had dragged the mummy nearer, and was examining it with the interest of a man whose ruling passion was strong even in death.

"'Come and help me unroll this. I have always longed to be the first to see and secure the curious treasures put away among the folds of these uncanny winding-sheets. This is a woman, and we may find something rare and precious here, ' he said, beginning to unfold the outer coverings, from which a strange aromatic odor came.

"Reluctantly I obeyed, for to me there was something sacred in the bones of this unknown woman. But to beguile the time and amuse the poor fellow, I lent a hand, wondering as I worked, if this dark, ugly thing had ever been a lovely, soft-eyed Egyptian girl.

"From the fibrous folds of the wrappings dropped precious gums and spices, which half intoxicated us with their potent breath, antique coins, and a curious jewel or two, which Niles eagerly examined.

"All the bandages but one were cut off at last, and a small head laid bare, round which still hung great plaits of what had once been luxuriant hair. The shriveled hands were folded on the breast, and clasped in them lay that gold box. "

"Ah! " cried Evelyn, dropping it from her rosy palm with a shudder.

"Nay; don't reject the poor little mummy's treasure. I never have quite forgiven myself for stealing it, or for burning her, " said Forsyth, painting rapidly, as if the recollection of that experience lent energy to his hand.

"Burning her! Oh, Paul, what do you mean? " asked the girl, sitting up with a face full of excitement.

"I'll tell you. While busied with Madame la Momie, our fire had burned low, for the dry case went like tinder. A faint, far-off sound made our hearts leap, and Niles cried out: 'Pile on the wood; Jumal is tracking us; don't let the smoke fail now or we are lost! '

"'There is no more wood; the case was very small, and is all gone, ' I answered, tearing off such of my garments as would burn readily, and piling them upon the embers.

"Niles did the same, but the light fabrics were quickly consumed, and made no smoke.

"'Burn that! ' commanded the professor, pointing to the mummy.

"I hesitated a moment. Again came the faint echo of a horn. Life was dear to me. A few dry bones might save us, and I obeyed him in silence.

"A dull blaze sprung up, and a heavy smoke rose from the burning mummy, rolling in volumes through the low passages, and threatening to suffocate us with its fragrant mist. My brain grew dizzy, the light danced before my eyes, strange phantoms seemed to people the air, and, in the act of asking Niles why he gasped and looked so pale, I lost consciousness. "

Evelyn drew a long breath, and put away the scented toys from her lap as if their odor oppressed her.

Forsyth's swarthy face was all aglow with the excitement of his story, and his black eyes glittered as he added, with a quick laugh:

"That's all; Jumal found and got us out, and we both forswore pyramids for the rest of our days. "

"But the box: how came you to keep it? " asked Evelyn, eyeing it askance as it lay gleaming in a streak of sunshine.

"Oh, I brought it away as a souvenir, and Niles kept the other trinkets. "

"But you said harm was foretold to the possessor of those scarlet seeds, " persisted the girl, whose fancy was excited by the tale, and who fancied all was not told.

"Among his spoils, Niles found a bit of parchment, which he deciphered, and this inscription said that the mummy we had so ungallantly burned was that of a famous sorceress who bequeathed her curse to whoever should disturb her rest. Of course I don't believe that curse has anything to do with it, but it's a fact that Niles never prospered from that day. He says it's because he has never recovered from the fall and fright and I dare say it is so; but I sometimes wonder if I am to share the curse, for I've a vein of superstition in me, and that poor little mummy haunts my dreams still. "

A long silence followed these words. Paul painted mechanically and Evelyn lay regarding him with a thoughtful face. But gloomy fancies were as foreign to her nature as shadows are to noonday, and presently she laughed a cheery laugh, saying as she took up the box again:

"Why don't you plant them, and see what wondrous flower they will bear? "

"I doubt if they would bear anything after lying in a mummy's hand for centuries, " replied Forsyth, gravely.

"Let me plant them and try. You know wheat has sprouted and grown that was taken from a mummy's coffin; why should not these pretty seeds? I should so like to watch them grow; may I, Paul? "

"No, I'd rather leave that experiment untried. I have a queer feeling about the matter, and don't want to meddle myself or let anyone I love meddle with these seeds. They may be some horrible poison, or possess some evil power, for the sorceress evidently valued them, since she clutched them fast even in her tomb. "

"Now, you are foolishly superstitious, and I laugh at you. Be generous; give me one seed, just to learn if it will grow. See I'll pay for it, " and Evelyn, who now stood beside him, dropped a kiss on his forehead as she made her request, with the most engaging air.

But Forsyth would not yield. He smiled and returned the embrace with lover-like warmth, then flung the seeds into the fire, and gave her back the golden box, saying, tenderly:

"My darling, I'll fill it with diamonds or bonbons, if you please, but I will not let you play with that witch's spells. You've enough of your own, so forget the 'pretty seeds' and see what a Light of the Harem I've made of you. "

Evelyn frowned, and smiled, and presently the lovers were out in the spring sunshine reveling in their own happy hopes, untroubled by one foreboding fear.

II

"I have a little surprise for you, love, " said Forsyth, as he greeted his cousin three months later on the morning of his wedding day.

"And I have one for you, " she answered, smiling faintly.

"How pale you are, and how thin you grow! All this bridal bustle is too much for you, Evelyn. " he said, with fond anxiety, as he watched the strange pallor of her face, and pressed the wasted little hand in his.

"I am so tired, " she said, and leaned her head wearily on her lover's breast. "Neither sleep, food, nor air gives me strength, and a curious mist seems to cloud my mind at times. Mamma says it is the heat, but I shiver even in the sun, while at night I burn with fever. Paul, dear, I'm glad you are going to take me away to lead a quiet, happy life with you, but I'm afraid it will be a very short one. "

"My fanciful little wife! You are tired and nervous with all this worry, but a few weeks of rest in the country will give us back our blooming Eve again. Have you no curiosity to learn my surprise? " he asked, to change her thoughts.

The vacant look stealing over the girl's face gave place to one of interest, but as she listened it seemed to require an effort to fix her mind on her lover's words.

"You remember the day we rummaged in the old cabinet? "

"Yes, " and a smile touched her lips for a moment.

"And how you wanted to plant those queer red seeds I stole from the mummy? "

"I remember, " and her eyes kindled with sudden fire.

"Well, I tossed them into the fire, as I thought, and gave you the box. But when I went back to cover up my picture, and found one of those seeds on the rug, a sudden fancy to gratify your whim led me to send it to Niles and ask him to plant and report on its progress. Today I hear from him for the first time, and he reports that the seed has grown marvelously, has budded, and that he intends to take the first flower, if it blooms in time, to a meeting of famous scientific men, after which he will send me its true name and the plant itself. From his description, it must be very curious, and I'm impatient to see it. "

"You need not wait; I can show you the flower in its bloom, " and Evelyn beckoned with the mechante smile so long a stranger to her lips.

Much amazed, Forsyth followed her to her own little boudoir, and there, standing in the sunshine, was the unknown plant. Almost rank in their luxuriance were the vivid green leaves on the slender purple stems, and rising from the midst, one ghostly-white flower, shaped like the head of a hooded snake, with scarlet stamens like forked tongues, and on the petals glittered spots like dew.

"A strange, uncanny flower! Has it any odor? " asked Forsyth, bending to examine it, and forgetting, in his interest, to ask how it came there.

"None, and that disappoints me, I am so fond of perfumes, " answered the girl, caressing the green leaves which trembled at her touch, while the purple stems deepened their tint.

"Now tell me about it, " said Forsyth, after standing silent for several minutes.

"I had been before you, and secured one of the seeds, for two fell on the rug. I planted it under a glass in the richest soil I could find, watered it faithfully, and was amazed at the rapidity with which it grew when once it appeared above the earth. I told no-one, for I meant to surprise you with it; but this bud has been so long in blooming, I have had to wait. It is a good omen that it blossoms today, and as it is nearly white, I mean to wear it, for I've learned to love it, having been my pet for so long. "

"I would not wear it, for, in spite of its innocent color, it is an evil-looking plant, with its adder's tongue and unnatural dew. Wait till Niles tells us what it is, then pet it if it is harmless. "

"Perhaps my sorceress cherished it for some symbolic beauty—those old Egyptians were full of fancies. It was very sly of you to turn the tables on me in this way. But I forgive you, since in a few hours, I shall chain this mysterious hand forever. How cold it is! Come out into the garden and get some warmth and color for tonight, my love."

But when night came, no-one could reproach the girl with her pallor, for she glowed like a pomegranate-flower, her eyes were full of fire, her lips scarlet, and all her old vivacity seemed to have returned. A more brilliant bride never blushed under a misty veil, and when her lover saw her, he was absolutely startled by the almost unearthly beauty which transformed the pale, languid creature of the morning into this radiant woman.

They were married, and if love, many blessings, and all good gifts lavishly showered upon them could make them happy, then this young pair were truly blest. But even in the rapture of the moment that made her his, Forsyth observed how icy cold was the little hand he held, how feverish the deep color on the soft cheek he kissed, and what a strange fire burned in the tender eyes that looked so wistfully at him.

Blithe and beautiful as a spirit, the smiling bride played her part in all the festivities of that long evening, and when at last light, life and color began to fade, the loving eyes that watched her thought it but the natural weariness of the hour. As the last guest departed, Forsyth was met by a servant, who gave him a letter marked

"Haste. " Tearing it open, he read these lines, from a friend of the professor's:

"DEAR SIR—Poor Niles died suddenly two days ago, while at the Scientific Club, and his last words were: 'Tell Paul Forsyth to beware of the Mummy's Curse, for this fatal flower has killed me. ' The circumstances of his death were so peculiar, that I add them as a sequel to this message. For several months, as he told us, he had been watching an unknown plant, and that evening he brought us the flower to examine. Other matters of interest absorbed us till a late hour, and the plant was forgotten. The professor wore it in his buttonhole— a strange white, serpent-headed blossom, with pale glittering spots, which slowly changed to a glittering scarlet, till the leaves looked as if sprinkled with blood. It was observed that instead of the pallor and feebleness which had recently come over him, that the professor was unusually animated, and seemed in an almost unnatural state of high spirits. Near the close of the meeting, in the midst of a lively discussion, he suddenly dropped, as if smitten with apoplexy. He was conveyed home insensible, and after one lucid interval, in which he gave me the message I have recorded above, he died in great agony, raving of mummies, pyramids, serpents, and some fatal curse which had fallen upon him.

"After his death, livid scarlet spots, like those on the flower, appeared upon his skin, and he shriveled like a withered leaf. At my desire, the mysterious plant was examined, and pronounced by the best authority one of the most deadly poisons known to the Egyptian sorceresses. The plant slowly absorbs the vitality of whoever cultivates it, and the blossom, worn for two or three hours, produces either madness or death. "

Down dropped the paper from Forsyth's hand; he read no further, but hurried back into the room where he had left his young wife. As if worn out with fatigue, she had thrown herself upon a couch, and lay there motionless, her face half-hidden by the light folds of the veil, which had blown over it.

"Evelyn, my dearest! Wake up and answer me. Did you wear that strange flower today? " whispered Forsyth, putting the misty screen away.

There was no need for her to answer, for there, gleaming spectrally on her bosom, was the evil blossom, its white petals spotted now with flecks of scarlet, vivid as drops of newly spilt blood.

But the unhappy bridegroom scarcely saw it, for the face above it appalled him by its utter vacancy. Drawn and pallid, as if with some wasting malady, the young face, so lovely an hour ago, lay before him aged and blighted by the baleful influence of the plant which had drunk up her life. No recognition in the eyes, no word upon the lips, no motion of the hand—only the faint breath, the fluttering pulse, and wide-opened eyes, betrayed that she was alive.

Alas for the young wife! The superstitious fear at which she had smiled had proved true: the curse that had bided its time for ages was fulfilled at last, and her own hand wrecked her happiness for ever. Death in life was her doom, and for years Forsyth secluded himself to tend with pathetic devotion the pale ghost, who never, by word or look, could thank him for the love that outlived even such a fate as this.

THE END

Printed in the United States
106371LV00002B/75/A

9 781406 597912